THE STORY OF
A LAMB ON WHEELS

LAURA LEE HOPE

Copyright © 2023 Culturea Editions
Text and cover : © public domain
Edition : Culturea (Hérault, 34)
Contact : infos@culturea.fr
Print in Germany by Books on Demand
Design and layout : Derek Murphy
Layout : Reedsy (https://reedsy.com/)
ISBN : 9791041828609
Légal deposit : July 2023

The Story Of A Lamb On Wheels

CHAPTER I

THE LAMB'S WISH

Out of his box the Jack popped his head. The funny, black fringe of whiskers around his face jiggled up and down. His queer, big eyes looked around the store.

"Hurray!" cried the Jack in the Box. "We are alone at last and now we can have some fun! Hurray!"

"Are you sure?" asked a Bold Tin Soldier, who stood at the head of a company of his men in a large box.

"Am I sure of what?" inquired the Jack, as he swung to and fro on the spring which made him pop out of the box.

"Are you sure we are alone?" went on the Soldier. "It would be too bad if we should come to life when any one could see us."

"There is no one in the department but us toys," said a Calico Clown, and he banged together some shiny cymbals on the ends of his arms. "The Jack is right—we are all by ourselves."

"I am glad of it," said a woolly Lamb on Wheels, who stood on the floor, just under the edge of the toy counter. She was rather too large to be up among the smaller toys. "Yes, I am glad of it," went on the Lamb. "I have kept still all day, and now I have something to tell you all, my friends."

"Something nice?" asked a Candy Rabbit, who stood next to a Monkey on a

Stick.

"I think it is nice," said the Lamb. "But, as you know, I could not move about or speak so long as any of the clerks or customers were here."

"That's so," agreed the Bold Tin Soldier.

For it was one of the rules of Toyland, as you know, that none of the folk who lived there could do anything while human eyes were watching them. The Dolls, Soldiers, Clowns, Rocking Horses, Lambs were not able to move, talk, or make believe come to life if a boy or a girl or any one at all looked at them.

"But now we are alone we can have some fun," said the Jack in the Box. "Let's have a jumping race, to see who can go the farthest. Come on! I'm ready!"

"Yes, you are always ready to jump out of your box as soon as the cover is taken off," remarked the Lamb on Wheels. "But the rest of us are not such high kickers as you are. I cannot jump at all. I can only run around on my wheels, just as the White Rocking Horse, who used to live here, could only go on his rockers."

"Well, what shall we do then?" asked the Jack. "I'm ready to do anything."

"Suppose we have the Calico Clown play us a little tune on his cymbals," suggested the Bold Tin Soldier. "My men and I like to hear his music. After that we will march around and then—"

"Then we must listen to what the Lamb has to say," cried the Monkey on a

Stick. "She said she had something to tell us."

"Oh, excuse me," came from the Bold Tin Soldier Captain, with a wave of his shiny sward. "Perhaps you want to tell us your story now, Miss Lamb?"

"No," she answered. "Later will do. It is not exactly a story—it is more of a wish. But first I should like to listen to the Calico Clown."

"All right! Here we go!" cried the jolly Clown. He was a gaily dressed fellow, and his calico suit was of many colors. One leg was red and another yellow, and his shirt was spotted and speckled and striped.

The Calico Clown stood up near the box where the Bold Tin Soldier was ready to lead his men in a march. And the Clown banged together his shiny cymbals.

"Bang! Bung! Bang! Bung!" clanged the cymbals, making music that the Toy Folk liked to hear, though I cannot say you would have cared much for it.

"Now it is your turn to march, Captain!" called the Candy Rabbit. "Show us what you and your men can do. That will amuse us." "All right!" agreed the Bold Tin Soldier. "Attention, men!" he cried, "Ready! Shoulder arms! Forward—March!"

Out of their box, following their Captain, came the tin soldiers. Around and around the toy counter they marched, the Calico Clown making music for them on his cymbals.

"Isn't this jolly!" cried the Monkey on a Stick.

Once more around the toy counter marched the Bold Tin Soldier and his men. They were careful not to get too near the edge, for they did not want to fall off.

"There, how did you like it?" asked the Captain, as his men stopped to rest.

"It was fine!" answered the Candy Rabbit. "Now we will listen to the

Lamb on Wheels."

"Oh, I'm sure I haven't so very much to say," said the white, fuzzy toy.

"But I was thinking, to-day, of the Sawdust Doll, and—"

"Do you mean the Sawdust Doll who used to live here with us?" asked the Calico Clown. "Excuse me for interrupting you," he said politely, "but I just couldn't help it. I was thinking of the Sawdust Doll myself. And I was wondering if you meant the same one that used to be here."

"Yes," answered the Lamb, "I did. It was of her I was thinking. She was on our toy counter about the same time the White Rocking Horse lived with us."

"And she went away just before he did," said the Monkey on a Stick. "The

Sawdust Doll comes back, once in a while, to see us. But the Rocking

Horse does not."

"It is harder for him than for her," said the Lamb. "The little girl, whose mother bought the Sawdust Doll, often brings her back to see us. And the Sawdust Doll once told me she had a lovely home with a little girl named Dorothy."

"And I think I heard her say that the White Rocking Horse lived in the same house with her, and belonged to a boy named Dick," said the Bold Tin Soldier.

"Yes, that is true," said the Lamb. "Well, what I was going to tell you about was a little girl who came in to look at me to-day. She was one of the nicest little girls I ever saw—fully as nice as the Dorothy who has the Sawdust Doll."

"And did this little girl buy you—or did her mother?" asked the Calico Clown. "I should hate to see you leave us," he went on. "Of course we want you to get a nice home, but it will be lonesome if you, too, go away." "That's so," said the Bold Tin Soldier. "We have lost our Sawdust Doll and our White Rocking Horse, and now, if the Lamb on Wheels goes away from us—dear me!"

"I have no idea of going away!" answered the Lamb. "All I was going to say was that a beautiful little girl came to the toy department to-day with her mother, and she admired me very much—the little girl did. She patted my back so softly, and she rubbed my head and she asked her mother to buy me."

"And did she?" asked the Calico Clown.

"No, I think not," replied the Lamb. "At least, if she did, I was not taken away. But I wish, oh, how I wish I could get into a nice home, such as the Sawdust Doll has."

"I trust you will get your wish," said the Calico Clown. "And I think we all have the same wish—that we will have kind boys and girls to own us when we go from here. But now let us be jolly. I'll tell you a funny riddle."

"Oh, yes, please do!" begged the Lamb. "I love riddles!"

"Let me see, now," mused the Calico Clown, softly banging together his cymbals. "I think I'll ask you the riddle about the pig. What makes more noise than a pig under a gate?"

"What kind of gate?" asked the Monkey on a Stick.

"It doesn't make any difference what kind of gate," said the Clown.

"I should think it would," the Monkey stated. "And while you are about it, why don't you tell us what kind of pig it is?"

"That doesn't make any difference either," said the Clown. "The riddle is what makes more noise than a pig under a gate."

"Excuse me, but I should think it would make a great deal of difference," went on the Monkey. "A big pig under a small gate would make more noise than a little pig under a big gate. If we only knew the size of the gate and what kind of pig it was, we might guess the riddle."

"Hark! I hear a noise! Some one is coming!" cried the Bold Tin Soldier, and all the toys became as quiet as mice.

CHAPTER II

THE JOLLY SAILOR

The noise which the toys had heard, and which had made them all stop talking, causing them to become as quiet as mice—this noise seemed to be coming nearer and nearer. It was a rolling, rumbling sort of noise.

"Can that be the watchman?" whispered the Calico Clown to the Bold Tin

Soldier.

"I hardly think so," was the answer. "He tramps along differently, his feet making a noise like the beat of a drum. This is quite another sound. But we had better keep still until we see what it is."

So all the toys kept quiet, and the noise came nearer and nearer and nearer, and then, all of a sudden, there rolled along the floor a toy Elephant on roller skates.

"Hello! Hello there, my toy friends!" cried the Elephant through his trunk. "How are you all? And where is the White Rocking Horse? I'll have a race with him. I tried to the other night, but one of my roller skates jiggled off and then the watchman came and the race could not be run. Where is the Rocking Horse?"

"Why, didn't you hear?" asked the Clown, as he sat up, for the toys knew it would be all right now to move about and talk as they had been doing.

"Didn't I hear what?" asked the Elephant, sliding around on his roller skates. "I hear a lot of things," he went on, "but these skates make so much racket I can't hear very well when I have them on. They don't really belong to me," he said, looking at the Candy Rabbit. "I just borrowed them from the sporting section, as I did before, to race with the White Rocking Horse."

"Well, you might have saved yourself the trouble," said the Monkey on a

Stick. "The White Rocking Horse isn't here any more. He was sold."

"Dear me!" exclaimed the Elephant. "That's too bad! Then I can't have a race."

"Unless you want to race with the Lamb on Wheels," said the Bold Tin

Soldier. "She has wheels on her feet almost like your roller skates.

Will you race with her?"

"Thank you, I don't believe I care to race," put in the Lamb. "I am not used to it. And I might break a leg, and then that nice little girl, who was petting me to-day, would not want to buy me. I had better not race."

"Just as you like," came from the Elephant. "But I am sorry that my friend, the White Rocking Horse, has gone. I wonder if I shall ever see him again."

And the Elephant did see the Rocking chap later on, as you may read in the book telling "The Story of the White Rocking Horse." It was in a Toy Hospital where they met, after each had had many adventures.

"Well, if we are not going to have a race, what shall we do?" asked the

Calico Clown.

"Suppose you tell us another riddle," said the Bold Tin Soldier.

"Let the Monkey on a Stick, the Jack in the Box and the Candy Rabbit have a jumping race!" proposed the Lamb. "They are all good jumpers."

"Oh, yes!" cried all the other toys. "A jumping race would be fine!"

"I'm ready!" said the Jack in the Box, waving to and fro on the end of his long, slender spring.

"So am I," said the Monkey, as he climbed to the top of his stick.

"Well, I suppose I shall have to do my best," said the Candy Rabbit.

"Clear a place on the counter, and we'll try some jumps."

The Bold Tin Soldier and his men soon cleared a place on the toy counter so that the Jack, the Monkey and the Rabbit would have plenty of room. The building blocks, the checkers and the dominoes were moved out of the way, and then the Calico Clown took his place, ready to count "One! Two! Three!" so the three toys would know when it was time to jump.

"I'm allowed to come out of my box, am I not?" asked the Jack.

"Oh, of course," said the Lamb on Wheels. "It would not be fair to have you jump and carry your box with you. You may come out."

So the Jack jumped out of his box and took his place next to the Monkey, who also came down off his stick. I wish you could have seen how nimble they were, but, really, it is not allowed. The minute you looked at any of the toys they stopped moving at once.

"Are you all ready?" asked the Calico Clown, banging his cymbals together. "If so—go!"

Away jumped the Candy Rabbit! Away jumped the Monkey! Away leaped the

Jack who lived in a Box. At the far end of the toy counter the Bold Tin

Soldier and his men had placed some sofa cushions from the upholstery

department. That was in case either of the three might stumble and fall.

"Look at the Jack jump!" exclaimed the Calico Clown.

"And see the Monkey sail through air," remarked the Lamb on Wheels.

"But the Candy Rabbit is doing best of all," said the Bold Tin Soldier.

And really the Rabbit was the best jumper of the three. In fact, he jumped so far that he sailed over the edge of the counter. And only that a sofa cushion fell, at the same time, to the floor, so that the Candy Rabbit landed on the soft, feathery thing, he might have hurt himself.

"The Candy Rabbit wins! The Candy Rabbit wins the jumping race!" cried the Calico Clown, banging together his cymbals.

"Yes, he is the best jumper," agreed the Monkey and the Jack, who had jumped only to the end of the toy counter.

"Oh, I'm sure you two could do as well if you had only had more practice," said the Candy Rabbit, who was a nice, modest sort of chap.

"Shall we try it again?" asked the Jack, who really thought he was a fine jumper.

"There will not be time," said the Bold Tin Soldier. "I can see the sun coming up. Soon the store will begin to fill with clerks and shoppers, and we must lie as still and quiet as if we never had moved or talked. To-morrow night we shall have more fun."

A little later the girls and young ladies who worked at the toy counters and shelves came in to get ready for customers.

Soon the people began coming in to look at the toys. The Lamb on Wheels stood on the floor just under the counter. She was rather a large lamb, over a foot high—that is, she was large for a toy lamb, though of course real ones are larger than that when they grow up.

"I wonder if I shall see that nice little girl to-day," thought the

Lamb, as she heard the hum and buzz of the shoppers. "I hope I may. And

I hope I get as nice a home as the Sawdust Doll has."

She stood up straight and stiff, on her legs, did the Lamb. Her feet were fast to a wooden platform, and under that were wheels, so the Lamb could be rolled along from place to place. At night, when no one was looking at her, the Lamb could move along on the wheels by herself. But now she was very still and quiet, staring straight ahead as the dolls stared.

"I wonder what will happen to me to-day," thought the Lamb on Wheels again.

Through the toy department came striding a jolly-looking man who, when he walked, seemed to swing from side to side.

"What ho!" cried the jolly man, as he stopped at the toy counter. "I want to buy something!" he added. "I'm a sailor, just back from a long sea voyage, and I have plenty of money! I want to buy a toy!"

"What kind of toy?" asked the girl behind the counter. "We have many kinds here," and she smiled at the sailor. He was so jolly no one could help smiling at him. "We have Bold Tin Soldiers," went on the girl. "We have Calico Clowns, Candy Rabbits, a Monkey on a Stick, and a Lamb on Wheels, and lots of things."

"Hum! those are all very nice toys," said the jolly sailor. "But I think

I'd like to look at the Lamb on Wheels."

"There she is, right in front of you, on the floor," said the girl.

"Oh, ho! So this is the Lamb on Wheels!" cried the jolly sailor as he picked her up. "Well, this seems just the toy I want. I'll take her! I'll buy this Lamb on Wheels!"

"Oh, dear me!" thought the Lamb, for she knew what was going on, even though she dared not move by herself, or speak, "if this sailor buys me he'll take me on an ocean trip and I'll be seasick! Oh, dear, this is going to be dreadful!"

CHAPTER III

A HOME ON SHORE

The jolly sailor held in his hands the Lamb on Wheels. He looked her over carefully, and rubbed her warm, woolly sides. Though his hand was not as soft as was that of the little girl who had stroked the Lamb the day before, yet the sailor was gentle in his touch.

"Well, I suppose there is no use thinking any longer of having a home like the one the Sawdust Doll got, with her little girl mistress to love her," said the Lamb on Wheels to herself. "I am to be taken away by this sailor—away out to sea. I never could stand sailing, anyhow. Oh, dear! why do I have to go?"

"Does she squeak?" asked the sailor of the clerk, as he held the Lamb in his hands.

"Oh, no. She isn't that kind of Lamb," answered the clerk, with a laugh. "She is just a Lamb on Wheels, and she has real wool on her back and sides and legs. She does not squeak or go baa-a-a-a, and if you want her to move you have to pull her along."

"Well, I was going to get a Lamb that squeaked," went on the sailor, "but I suppose this one will do just as well."

"We have a Calico Clown who bangs his cymbals together when you press on his stomach or chest," said the girl. "See this toy! Maybe you would like this!"

She picked up the Calico Clown in his gaily colored suit, and, pressing on him in the middle, she made him bang his cymbals together.

"That is a jolly toy," said the sailor. "Let me see it."

He took up the Calico Clown, and did as the girl clerk had done.

"Bing! Bang! Bung!" went the cymbals.

"Oh, I hope he buys me," thought the Clown. "I should love to go to sea on a ship."

But the sailor appeared to like the Lamb on Wheels best. He took her up again, and the Lamb, who had begun to hope that she might not have to go to sea, felt sad again.

"I'll take this Lamb on Wheels," said the sailor. "How much is it?" and he pulled out his pocketbook, as he tucked the lamb under his arm.

"Oh, I must wrap it up for you," said the girl. "You are not supposed to take things from the store unless they are wrapped. I'll get a large piece of paper for the Lamb."

And while the clerk was gone the sailor walked about, looking at some bicycles and velocipedes at the far end of the toy department. Thus the Lamb and her friends were left by themselves for a moment or two, with no one to look at them. This was just the chance the Lamb wanted. She could talk now.

"Oh, just think of where I am going to be taken!" she said to the Calico

Clown. "Off to sea!"

"Real jolly, I call it!" said the Clown. "I wish he had picked me for the trip."

"And I wish he had taken me," put in the Bold Tin Soldier. "I have always longed for a sea trip."

"Well, I wish either of you had gone in my place," said the Lamb on

Wheels, a bit sadly. "Now I shall never see the Sawdust Doll or the

White Rocking Horse again."

"You must make the best of it," said the Monkey on a Stick. "I know what sailors are—I have heard of them. They like to have monkeys and parrots for pets—that is, real ones, not toys such as we are. But sailors are kind, I have heard."

But the woolly Lamb only sighed. She felt certain that she would be seasick, and no one can have a good time thinking of that.

"Well, if you go on an ocean trip we may never see you again," said the

Monkey on a Stick. "Ocean travel is very dangerous."

"Nonsense! It isn't anything of the sort!" cried the Calico Clown, and he tried to wink at the Monkey from behind a pile of building blocks. "The ocean is as safe as the shore. Why, look at the English and French dolls," he said, waving his cymbals in the direction of the imported toys in the next aisle. "They came over the ocean in a ship, and they did not even have a headache. And look at the Japanese dolls—they came much farther, over another ocean, too, and their hair was not even mussed."

"That's so," said the Lamb, and she felt a little better at hearing this.

"You want to keep still—don't scare her!" whispered the Clown to the

Monkey. "It's bad enough as it is—having her taken away by the sailor.

Don't make it worse!"

"All right, I won't," said the Monkey. And he began to talk about the happier side of an ocean trip; how beautiful the sunset was, and how there was never any dust at sea.

Then the sailor came back from having looked at the velocipedes, and the girl clerk brought a large sheet of paper. In this the Lamb was wrapped. She had a last look at her friends of the toy shelves and counters, and then she felt herself being lifted up by the sailor.

Out of the store the sailor carried the Lamb on Wheels. She wished she had had time to say good-bye to her friends, but she had not, and she must make the best of it.

"At any rate I am going to have adventures, even though they may be on a ship, and even though I may be seasick," thought the Lamb. "And perhaps I may not be so very ill."

On and on walked the sailor, down this street up another until, after a while, he stopped in front of a house.

"This must be the place," he said to himself. "I wonder if Mirabell is at home. I'll go in and see."

Up the steps he went and rang the bell. There was a hole in the paper wrapped about the Lamb, and through this hole she could look out. She saw that she was on the piazza of a fine, large house. There was another house next door, and at the window stood a little girl with a doll in her arms.

"Gracious goodness!" exclaimed the Lamb on Wheels to herself. "That looks just like the Sawdust Doll who used to live in our store! I wonder if it could be?"

However she had no further chance to look, for the door opened just then, and the sailor went inside the house, carrying the Lamb with him.

"Where's Mirabell?" asked the sailor of the maid who opened the door.

"She is up in the playroom," was the answer. "She has been ill, but she is better now."

"So I heard!" went on the jolly sailor. "I brought her something to look at. That will help her to get well."

Up to the playroom he went, and no sooner had he opened the door than

Mirabell, which was the name of the little girl, ran toward him.

"Oh, Uncle Tim!" cried Mirabell, as soon as she saw the jolly sailor, "how glad I am to see you!"

"And I'm glad to see you, Mirabell," he laughed. "Look, I have brought you something!"

"Is it a monkey, Uncle Tim?" she asked.

"No, Mirabell, it isn't a monkey. It is a woolly Lamb on Wheels. I saw it in a toy store and I brought it to you."

"For me—to keep, Uncle Tim?" asked Mirabell, as the sailor took the wrapping paper off.

"Yes, for you to keep," was the sailor's answer. "Did you think I would be buying a Lamb for myself, to take to sea with me? Ho! Ho! I should say not!" he chuckled.

"Oh, how glad I am! And how I shall love this Lamb!" said the little girl.

As for the Lamb on Wheels, she was glad and happy, too, when she heard, as she did, what the sailor said.

"Oh, I'm to have a home on shore!" thought the Lamb. "I am not going to be taken on an ocean voyage at all, and be made seasick. I am to have a home on shore!"

And that is just what the toy Lamb had. The jolly sailor, who was

Mirabell's uncle, had bought the toy for the little girl.

"Do you like the Lamb?" asked Uncle Tim.

"Oh, do I? Well, I just guess I do!" cried Mirabell, and she hugged the

Lamb in her arms, and rolled her across the floor on her wheels.

"Do you know, Uncle Tim," went on Mirabell, "this is the very same Lamb

I saw in the store, and wanted so much?"

"No! Is she?" asked the sailor, in surprise.

"The very same one!" declared Mirabell. "I was in the store once with Dorothy, the little girl who lives next door. She has a Sawdust Doll that came from the same store. And we were there the other day, before I was taken ill, and I saw a woolly lamb—this very same one, I'm sure—and I wanted it so much! But Mother said I must wait, and I'm glad I did, for now you gave it to me."

"Yes, I'm giving you the Lamb for yourself—to keep forever," said the sailor. "I wouldn't dream of taking her on a sea voyage with me."

So you see the Lamb need not have been uneasy after all. But of course she did not know that when the sailor bought her.

Mirabell stroked the soft wool of her new toy Lamb. She wheeled it across the floor again, and the sailor watched her. Then, all of a sudden, the door of the playroom was opened with such a bang that it struck the Lamb and sent her spinning across the floor, upside down, into a corner.

"Oh, Arnold!" cried Mirabell to her brother, who had come in so roughly.

"Look what you did! You've broken my Lamb on Wheels!"

CHAPTER IV

SLIDING DOWNHILL

Arnold, who was a boy about as old as Dick, the brother of Dorothy, stopped short after slamming open the playroom door. He looked at his sister, then at the Lamb lying upside down in a corner, and then he looked at the jolly sailor.

"What did I do?" asked Arnold, who was taken by surprise by the way his sister called to him.

"You broke my new toy, the Lamb on Wheels," answered the little girl. "Oh, I hope she isn't killed!" and running to the corner, she picked up her new toy.

"Oh, I didn't mean to do that," said Arnold, who was sorry enough for the accident. "I didn't know you were in here," he went on. "I came to get my toy fire engine. I'm going to play with Dick and his express wagon. Where'd you get your Lamb on Wheels, Mirabell?"

"Uncle Tim brought her to me," answered the little girl.

Mirabell carefully looked at her plaything. And she was very glad to find out that no damage seemed to have been done. None of the four wheels was broken, the little wooden platform on which the Lamb stood was not splintered, and there was not so much as a bruise on the little black nose of the Lamb herself.

"I guess she is so soft and woolly that she didn't get hurt much," Mirabell said, turning the Lamb over and over. "She's so fat and soft—like a rubber ball," she added.

"I'm glad of that," said Arnold. "Next time I come into a room I'll look near the door to see that there isn't a Lamb behind it."

"That's the boy!" exclaimed Uncle Tim. "And here is something I brought for you, Arnold. I didn't buy it in a toy store. It's a little wooden puzzle I whittled with my knife out of a bit of wood when I was on the ship."

Arnold looked at what Uncle Tim gave him. It was a puzzle, made of some wooden rings on a stick, and the trick was to get the rings off the stick. Arnold tried and tried but could not do it until his uncle showed him how the trick was done. Then it was easy.

"Oh, thank you!" cried the boy, when he had learned how to do the trick himself. "I'm going over and show Dick this puzzle. I don't believe he can do it. Want to come, Mirabell, and show Dorothy your Lamb on Wheels?"

"No, thank you, not now," Arnold's sister answered. "I'm going to get a comb and brush and make my Lamb's wool all nice and fluffy. She got all mussed when you banged her into the corner."

"I'm sorry," said Arnold again. "Do you want me to brush her off for you?"

"I guess not!" laughed Mirabell. "Once you tried to get the tangles and snarls out of the hair of one of my dolls, and you 'most pulled her head off."

"All right. Then I'll take this puzzle and show it to Dick and Dorothy," decided Arnold.

"Who are Dick and Dorothy?" asked Uncle Tim.

"The little boy and girl who live next door," Mirabell explained. "Dorothy has a Sawdust Doll, and Dick has a White Rocking Horse. They came from the same store where you got my Lamb on Wheels!"

"Is that so?" cried the jolly sailor. "Well, you'll have to take your

Lamb over next door and let her meet her toy friends again."

"I'm going to," Dorothy said. "Oh, Uncle Tim, don't you believe Dolls, and Lambs, and things like that, really know one another when they meet?"

"I shouldn't be a bit surprised if they did," answered the sailor. "You take your Lamb over and see if she remembers the Sawdust Doll and the White Rocking Horse."

"I will!" promised Mirabell.

And when the Lamb heard this, though just then she dared not move by herself or speak, she felt very happy. For, as I have told you, though she dared not move when human eyes were looking at her, there was nothing to stop her from hearing what was said. The Lamb had ears, and what good would they be if she could not hear through them, I'd like to know?

"Oh, I am so glad I am going to see the Sawdust Doll and the Rocking Horse again," thought the Lamb. "I hope I get a chance to talk to them when no one is looking. I want to tell them about their friends that are still in the toy store."

While Arnold hurried next door with his toy fire engine, that pumped real water, to play with Dick and to show his puzzle, Uncle Tim went downstairs to talk to Mirabell's mother. Then Mirabell got her best doll's comb and brush, which were just the right size, and not a bit too small or too large, and with this comb and brush she smoothed the kinks and snarls out of the Lamb's wool.

For when Arnold had opened the door so suddenly, banging the Lamb into a corner, though he did not mean to do it, he had tangled the woolly coat of the toy.

"But I'll soon smooth it out," thought Mirabell, as she used comb and brush. "And I won't hurt you, either, my nice Lamb!"

And Mirabell was so careful that the Lamb never once cried Baa-a! as almost any other lamb would do if you pulled her wool.

The little girl had made her Lamb nice and tidy, and she was going downstairs, Mirabell was, to see what Uncle Tim was doing, when Arnold came back from Dick's house with the toy fire engine and the wooden puzzle the sailor had made for him.

"Oh, Mirabell, I know how we can have a lot of fun!" cried Arnold.

"How?" asked the little girl.

"With your new Lamb," went on her brother. "Come on, I'll show you. We must go down to the kitchen. It's a new trick. Dick told me about it. He did it with an old roller skate."

"What trick is it?" asked Mirabell. "I hope it won't hurt my Lamb."

"No, it'll be a lot of fun," said Arnold. "I told Dick and Dorothy about your Lamb, and they want to see her. I guess the Sawdust Doll and the Rocking Horse want to see her, too."

"I'll go over to-morrow," promised Mirabell. "Now show me the funny trick, Arnold."

The two children went down to the kitchen. There was no one in it just then, as the cook was out, and Mother was in the parlor talking to Uncle Tim, the sailor.

"First we've got to get the long ironing board," said Arnold.

"What are we going to do with that?" Mirabell asked.

"Make a sliding downhill thing for your Lamb," answered her brother.

"Why, how can you do that?" asked Mirabell. "There isn't any snow now, though there was some for Christmas. How can you make a sliding downhill thing without snow?"

"Ill show you," Arnold said. "Wait till I get the ironing board."

It was kept in the cellar-way, hanging on a nail, and Arnold went there to get it. But the board was so long and heavy that his sister had to help him lift it down off the nail.

"We'll put one end up on a chair, and the other end down on the floor," said Arnold. "That will make a sliding downhill place."

"Yes," replied Mirabell, as she saw her brother do this. "But it isn't slippery enough for anybody to slide down. You must have snow for a hill."

"Not this kind," Arnold answered, with a laugh. "You see your Lamb has wheels on her, and she can roll right down the ironing board hill, just like Dick made an old roller skate roll down. Look, Mirabell!"

Arnold took the Lamb from his sister's arms and set the toy on the high end of the slanting ironing-board hill. And when the Lamb looked down, and saw how steep it was, and how long, she said to herself:

"Oh, I'm afraid something dreadful will happen to me! I never coasted downhill before, though I have heard some of the sleds and toboggans in the toy department speak of it. Oh, he's letting go of me!" she cried to herself, as she felt Arnold taking off his hands by which he had been holding her at the top of the ironing-board hill. "He's going to let me go!"

And let go of the Lamb Arnold did.

"Watch her coast, Mirabell!" he called to his sister.

Slowly at first, the Lamb on Wheels began to roll down the long, smooth, sloping board. Then she began to go faster and faster. At the bottom she could see the shiny oilcloth on the kitchen floor. Beyond the end of the ironing board the kitchen floor stretched out a long way.

"Oh, I feel so queer!" bleated the Lamb as, faster and faster, she slid down the ironing-board hill. "Oh, what a strange adventure!"

CHAPTER V

IN GREAT DANGER

"Look, Mirabell!" cried Arnold, pointing to the Lamb as she went down the ironing board. "Didn't I tell you she could coast without any snow?"

"Yes, you did, and she really is doing it!" laughed the little girl, clapping her hands. "Oh, isn't it nice? I never thought a Lamb could coast downhill!"

"I never did, either," said the woolly Lamb to herself. "This is the first time I was ever made to do a thing like this, and I hope it will be the last! Oh, how fast I am going!"

"It's the wheels on her that make her coast so nice," explained Arnold, when the Lamb was half way down the ironing-board hill. "If she didn't have them she wouldn't roll down at all. A Sawdust Doll can't do it, nor a Rocking Horse. It's got to be something with wheels."

When the Lamb heard this, as, of course, she did hear, having ears, she thought to herself:

"Well, maybe this will not be so bad, after all. I can do things, it seems, that the Sawdust Doll and Rocking Horse cannot do. Not that I am going to be proud, or stuck up," went on the Lamb to herself.

"Oh, look at her go!" cried Dick.

"Yes, but I hope she won't be hurt," said the little girl. "I wouldn't want my Lamb on Wheels that Uncle Tim just gave me to be hurt."

"I should say not!" thought the Lamb to herself. "Sliding down ironing-board hills may be something not many other toys can do, but I don't want anything to happen."

Faster and faster she went, and finally she reached the end of the board and came to the smooth oilcloth on the floor. Then the wheels carried her across that to the far side of the room, and the Lamb brought up with a little bump against the baseboard.

"Oh, I hope she isn't hurt!" cried Mirabell, as she ran to pick up her toy.

And the Lamb was all right—there was not even a kink out of place in her soft, woolly coat.

So Mirabell and Arnold had fun letting the Lamb on Wheels coast down the ironing-board hill. Again and again they gave her a nice, long slide across the smooth oilcloth on the kitchen floor.

"Now this is the last," said Mirabell, after a while. "I want to put her to sleep."

Once more the Lamb was lifted to the high part of the ironing board and allowed to coast down on her wheels. But, alas! this time, just as she was rolling over the kitchen floor, one of the wheels hit against Arnold's foot. Instead of going in a straight line the Lamb swung off to one side. Straight toward the outside door she rolled, and just then Susan, the cook, came in from out-of-doors.

Susan held the door open for a moment, and before either Mirabell or

Arnold could stop the Lamb, out she rolled to the back steps.

"Oh, my Lamb! My Lamb!" cried Mirabell. "She'll break her legs if she falls down the steps!"

Down the back steps, bumpity-bump went the Lamb on Wheels. But she did not break any of her four legs, I am glad to say.

Just how it happened I do not know, but when Mirabell and Arnold ran out to pick up the Lamb on Wheels the children found that the toy was not in the least hurt, except, maybe, the wool was ruffled up a little.

"Dear me, what a lot of adventures I am having!" thought the Lamb, as

Mirabell picked her up. "I wish I could tell the Calico Clown or the

Bold Tin Soldier something about them. They are quite remarkable, I

think!"

"Is she hurt?" asked Arnold, as he saw his sister holding her new toy.

"No, she seems to be all right," replied Mirabell. "But I'm not going to slide her down the ironing-board hill any more to-day. She must go to sleep."

So the board was hung away, and soon the Lamb was put in a little stable Mirabell made for her out of a pasteboard box. The stable was set in a corner of the playroom, near a little Wooden Lion that had once lived in a Noah's Ark. He was the only one of the Ark animals left. Arnold or Mirabell had lost all the others.

"Don't be afraid of me! I won't bite you," said the Wooden Lion to the Lamb on Wheels, when they were left alone in the playroom. The children had gone downstairs to supper with Uncle Tim, and the sailor was telling them many jolly stories of the sea.

"Oh, I'm not afraid of you," said the Lamb on Wheels to the Wooden Lion.

"I am much larger than you, even if you are like the jungle animals."

"It isn't my fault that I am small," said the Wooden Lion, a little crossly, the Lamb thought. "I had to be made that way to fit in the Ark. You ought to see the Elephant. He isn't much larger than myself!"

"Did he have on roller skates?" asked the Lamb.

"Roller skates!" exclaimed the Wooden Lion. "Why! who ever heard of such a thing? A Noah's Ark Elephant on roller skates! The idea!"

"Oh, you needn't get so excited," said the Lamb, as she wiggled her short tail the least bit. "In the toy store, where I came from, we had an Elephant who put on roller skates and raced with a White Rocking Horse."

"I wish I could have seen that," said the little Wooden Lion. "It must have been funny."

"It was," said the Lamb on Wheels. "The Elephant wanted to race with me, after the Horse was taken away. But I was sold, too, and brought here."

"I am glad to see you," said the Noah's Ark Lion. "I have been quite lonesome. There used to be a number of us—there was a Tiger, a Camel, a Monkey, a Hippopotamus, and, oh! ever so many others, besides the Elephant. But we are all scattered. I am the only one left. Tell me, were you ever in a Noah's Ark?"

"I never was," admitted the Lamb. "Is it nice?"

"Well, yes, only it's a bit crowded," answered the Wooden Lion. "But it has to be that way, I suppose. I like it better in this playroom, as I can move about more. But still I was lonesome until you came. Let us be friends, and tell each other our adventures."

So the Lamb told of the fun she had had in the toy store with the Bold Tin Soldier, the Calico Clown, and the others. She told of having been taken away by the jolly sailor, and how afraid she was that she would be seasick.

"But it was all right when I found he was bringing me to a home on shore with Mirabell," said the Lamb. Then she told of her slide down the ironing board.

"Now I will tell you some of the things that happened to me," said the Wooden Lion. So he related his adventures—how once he and the other animals had been jumbled together and piled into the Ark.

"And then, all of a sudden, that boy Arnold took the Ark and dropped it in the bathtub full of water, with all us animals inside!" said the Lion.

"Good gracious! why did he do that?" asked the Lamb, in surprise.

"Oh, he said he was pretending there was another flood, and he wanted to see if any of us could swim," the Lion answered.

"Could you?" the Lamb wanted to know.

"Well, those of us who couldn't swim could float, so none of us was drowned," the Lion answered. "Only being soaked in the water, as I was, made some of the paint come off my tail. I really haven't been the same Lion since," he added, with a sorrowful sigh.

"That is too bad," said the Lamb sympathetically.

"Of course Arnold was smaller than he is now, and he was not so kind to his toys as he has since learned to be," resumed the Wooden Lion. "He really meant no harm. But, as I say, I am the only one of the Noah's Ark animals left, and really I am very glad to have you to talk to."

The two new friends spent some time together telling each other their different adventures, and then, suddenly, the door of the playroom opened and Mirabell came in.

"Hush! Not another word!" said the Wooden Lion in a whisper.

"Well, I guess my Lamb has slept long enough," said Mirabell, picking up her new toy. "I'll have some fun with her before I go to bed."

She petted her Lamb, and took off the blue ribbon from the woolly creature's neck.

"I must smooth it out and tie a better bow," said Mirabell. "It got all mussed when you slid down the ironing board."

So Mirabell played with her Lamb until it was time for the little girl to go to bed. Uncle Tim came up to see Mirabell and Arnold to say good-bye, for he was going on a sea voyage.

"And bring me a parrot when you come back!" begged Arnold.

"Would you like a monkey, Mirabell?" asked the jolly sailor.

"No, thank you," she answered. "A monkey is nice, but he might pull the wool off my Lamb."

"That's so—he might!" laughed the jolly sailor. "Well, good-bye,

Mirabell, Arnold, and the Lamb on Wheels."

Then Uncle Tim went away and the children went to bed, while the Lamb on Wheels was put in the pasteboard box stable, near the Wooden Lion. And in the night they played together and had a fine time.

The Lamb on Wheels, in the days that followed, began to feel quite at home in Mirabell's house, and she liked her little girl mistress better and better, for Mirabell was very kind.

"Some day, when it gets warmer, I'll take my Lamb over to Dorothy's house and let her see the Sawdust Doll," said Mirabell to her brother.

"And I'll take my fire engine over and I'll ride on Dick's Rocking Horse," said Arnold. "But it is so cold now the water in my engine might freeze if I took it over to Dick's house."

"Yes, it is cold," agreed Mirabell. "I guess I'll take my Lamb down to the sitting room, where there's a fire on the hearth."

"I'll come too," said Arnold. "I'll bring my little fire engine."

Soon the two children were having a good time with their toys in front of the fireplace in the sitting room. On the hearth blazed a snapping, crackling warm fire of logs.

"Now you can get nice and warm," said Mirabell to her Lamb, as she set her down close to the fireplace. "You stay here and get warm, and I'll go and ask Susan for some cookies to eat."

Arnold also went to the kitchen with his sister, and when the two children came back to the sitting room they saw a dreadful sight. A spark had popped out from the hearth and set fire to a piece of paper on the floor near the Lamb on Wheels.

"Oh, she'll burn! My Lamb on Wheels will burn!" cried Mirabell, as she rushed forward.

CHAPTER VI

DOWN THE COAL HOLE

Mirabell and Arnold had been told to be very careful whenever they played in the sitting room, if a fire were burning on the open hearth. But, for the moment, the little girl forgot about this. All she thought of was that her Lamb on Wheels might be burned by the blazing paper, which had been set on fire by a spark popping out from the blazing logs on the hearth.

"Oh, my Lamb! My poor Lamb!" cried Mirabell.

"Look out!" shouted Arnold. "Don't go too close!"

"Why not?" asked his sister. "I have to get my Lamb on Wheels away from the fire!"

"No, you mustn't!" Arnold said. "Your dress might catch on fire!"

The piece of paper was burning on the wide brick hearth of the fireplace, and not on the carpet, and the Lamb was close to the piece of paper that was on fire. Altogether too close to the fire was the Lamb. She was in great danger.

"But I've got to save her! I must save my pet Lamb!" cried Mirabell. She was going to rush forward, but her brother caught hold of her and held her back.

"Wait!" cried Arnold. "I can put out the fire and save your Lamb."

"How!"

"With my fire engine! It has real water in it, and I'll pump some on the paper and save your Lamb from burning up. Watch me, Mirabell, but don't go near the blaze!"

The piece of paper, close to the Lamb on Wheels, was now sending up a bright blaze. It would have been pretty if it had not been so dangerous.

Arnold quickly wheeled his fire engine as close to the blazing paper as he felt it was safe to go. The engine had a little pump on it, as I have told you, and it spurted out real water, with which it was now filled.

"Toot! Toot! I'm a fireman, and I'm going to put out a real fire!" cried

Arnold.

He pressed back the little catch that held the pump from working. There was a whirring sound as the wheels spun around, and then the little rubber hose on the pump of the engine filled with water.

A moment later a small stream spurted out, and Arnold aimed it right for the piece of blazing paper. The water fell in a small shower on the fire, and then with a hiss and spluttering, and sending up a cloud of smoke, the paper stopped burning.

"Toot! Toot! The fire is out!" cried the boy, making believe blow his engine whistle. "Now your Lamb is saved, Mirabell."

"Oh, I'm so glad! Thank you, Arnold!" exclaimed his sister.

She ran forward and picked up her Lamb on Wheels. And, I am glad to say, the wool was not even scorched, not the least, tiny bit.

"Oh, she's all right! She's all right! My Lamb isn't hurt a bit,

Arnold," cried Mirabell.

"I told you I'd save her," said the boy. "But you mustn't ever run near a fire yourself, Mirabell. Wait for me to put it out with my engine. That's what fire engines and fire departments are for."

"Dear me! that came near being a terrible adventure for me," thought the Lamb on Wheels, as Mirabell carried her back from the fireplace. "In another minute I would have been all ablaze from that paper, and wool does burn so fast!"

When the Lamb had been saved, the mother of the two children came into the sitting room.

"What is burning?" she cried. "Have you been playing with fire?"

"No, Mother," answered Arnold, and he told what had happened.

As the days passed Mirabell came to love her Lamb on Wheels more and more. Sometimes the little girl would tie a string to the wooden platform, on which her toy stood, and pull the Lamb around the house, as Arnold used to pull his little express wagon.

"I like to ride that way," thought the Lamb. "It is much more fun than it would be to be crowded into a Noah's Ark like the Wooden Lion and thrown into the flooded bathtub."

The Lamb was wishing Mirabell would take her next door, to see the Sawdust Doll, but, as it happened, Dorothy was ill, and it was not thought best for Mirabell to go in for a few days. However, Mirabell could look from her windows over to those in the house where Dick and Dorothy lived. And though Dorothy was too ill to be out of bed, Dick was not.

Dick would stand at the window in his house, and Mirabell and Arnold would stand at the window in their front room, and look across. The children waved to one another, and Dick would hold up the head of his Rocking Horse for Mirabell and Arnold to see.

Once Mirabell held up her Lamb on Wheels at the same time that Dick had his Rocking Horse close to the window, and the two toys saw each other for the first time since they had been separated.

"Oh, there is my old friend, the White Rocking Horse!" thought the Lamb on Wheels. "How I wish I could talk to him."

The Horse wished the same thing, and he even thought perhaps he might get a chance to run over some evening after dark and talk to the Lamb. But the doors of both houses were locked each night, and though the Horse and Lamb could roam about and seem to come to life when no one was watching them, they could not unlock doors. So they had to be content to look at each other through the windows.

"I wish I could see the Sawdust Doll," thought the Lamb, when she had looked over at the Horse one day. "I'd like to speak to her."

There came a few days of bright sunshine, when the weather was not so cold. One afternoon Arnold said to Mirabell:

"I'm going to take my little express wagon out on the sidewalk in front of the house. Why don't you bring out your Lamb?"

"I will, if Mother will let me," said Mirabell.

And Mother did. Soon the two children were running up and down in front of the house, Mirabell pulling her Lamb along by a string, and Arnold pretending to be an expressman with his wagon.

"Oh, there comes a man to put some coal in Dorothy's house!" called

Arnold, as a big wagon, drawn by two strong horses, stopped in front of

the place where the Sawdust Doll and the White Rocking Horse lived.

"Let's go down and watch!" he said.

"All right," agreed Mirabell. So she pulled her Lamb on Wheels down the sidewalk, and Arnold hauled his express wagon along.

At Dorothy's house the coal bin was partly under the pavement, and to put in coal a round, iron cover was lifted up from a hole in the sidewalk, and the coal was dumped through this hole. As the children watched, and as

Dorothy, who was now better, stood at the window with her brother Dick, also looking on, the coal man took the cover off the hole in the sidewalk, so he could dump the black lumps through the opening into the bin.

"I wouldn't want to fall down there!" said Mirabell to her brother.

"I should say not!" exclaimed Arnold. "You'd get all black!"

The coal man, after opening the large, round hole in the sidewalk, climbed back on his wagon to shovel off his load. And just then Carlo, the dog belonging to Dorothy, ran barking out of the side entrance of the house where he lived. Carlo always became excited when coal was being put in the sidewalk hole.

"Bow-wow! Wow!" barked Carlo.

"Look out you don't fall down the hole!" cried Mirabell.

Just then Carlo gave a jump around behind the little girl, and, somehow or other, he became entangled in the string that was tied on the Lamb.

"Look out, Carlo! Look out!" cried Mirabell. "Be careful or you'll break my Lamb's string!"

But Carlo was not careful. He did not mean to make trouble, but he did. He barked and growled and jumped around until his legs were all tangled up in the cord.

"Oh, look!" suddenly cried Arnold. "Look at your Lamb!"

And, as he spoke, Carlo gave a big jump to get the tangling string off his legs. The string broke, but, as it did so, the Lamb started to roll toward the open coal hole. And, at the same moment, the driver of the wagon began shoveling some of the black lumps down the opening.

"Oh! Oh! Oh!" cried Mirabell.

And then the white, woolly Lamb on Wheels rolled across the sidewalk, and disappeared down into the dark coal hole!

CHAPTER VII

THE LAMB CARRIED AWAY

Mirabell and Arnold were so surprised for a moment at what had happened that they could only stand, looking at the hole in the sidewalk down which the Lamb on Wheels had fallen. Carlo, the fuzzy little dog, seemed to know he had done something wrong in getting tangled in the string, breaking it off, and so sending the Lamb wheeling along until she slid into the coal hole. And the dog gave a howl and ran back toward the house, having finally managed to get his legs loose from the cord.

"Bow-wow!" barked Carlo, as he ran.

Perhaps he feared that he, too, might slip down that black, dark hole which led into the coal bin of Dorothy's house. Then as Mirabell and Arnold stood, looking with wide-opened eyes at the place where they had last seen the Lamb, the man on the wagon threw another shovelful of coal down the hole.

"Wait a minute! Stop! Oh, please stop!" begged Mirabell.

"Whut's dat? Whut's de mattah?" asked the coal-wagon driver.

He was a colored man, and that was the very best shade for him, I think.

No matter how much coal dust got on his face and hands it never showed.

"Her little Lamb fell down the coal hole," explained Arnold. "Carlo got tangled in the string, it broke and she fell down the hole. Don't throw any more coal on her until we get her out."

"Does you-all mean dat Carlo fell down de hole?" asked the colored coal-wagon driver.

"No, Carlo is a dog," explained Mirabell. "He got tangled up in my

Lamb's string, and she fell down the hole. I haven't named my Lamb yet.

She's on wheels."

"On wheels?" cried the man. "A Lamb on Wheels? Well, I 'clar to goodness dat's de fustest time I ebber done heah ob a t'ing laik dat!"

"Oh, she isn't a real, live lamb," explained Mirabell. "She's a toy, woolly one from the store, and my Uncle Tim, who's a sailor, gave her to me."

"Well now, honey, I suah is sorry to heah dat!" said the colored man.

"Your toy Lamb down de coal hole! Dat is too bad!"

"Can we get her out?" asked Arnold. "I'll crawl down the hole and get the Lamb if you won't throw any more coal."

"Oh, I won't frow any mo' coal—not fo' a while—not when I knows whut de trouble is," said the kind-hearted driver. "But I doan believe, mah li'l man, dat you'd better go down de coal hole."

At that moment the door of Dorothy's house opened, and her mother came out on the porch.

"What is it, Mirabell?" she asked. "What has happened?" She saw the children from next door talking to the coal driver, and she wondered at it.

"Oh, my Lamb is down the coal hole!" said Mirabell.

"Oh, that's too bad!" exclaimed Dorothy's mother. "I saw you holding a toy Lamb up to the window, before Dorothy was taken ill. How did your toy get down the coal hole?"

Mirabell and Arnold told by turns, and the driver said:

"I suah is sorry, lady. But it w'an't mahfaulta-tall!"

"I know it wasn't," said Dorothy's mother. "But do you think you could get the little girl's Lamb's back?"

"Well, dat coal hole isn't so very big," was the answer, as the driver scratched his kinky head. "But I might squeeze mahse'f down in it."

"Oh, I think a better way would be to go down in our cellar, crawl over the bin, and get the Lamb that way," Dorothy's mother said.

"Yes-sum, I could do it dat way!" the colored man said. "I'se been down in yo' cellar befo'. I'll get de Lamb on Wheels."

Dorothy's mother waited on the front porch, and Mirabell and Arnold waited on the sidewalk near the coal hole. A little while after the colored man had gone in the side entrance, through the cellar and into the coal bin, the two children heard him calling, as if from the ground beneath them.

"I got de Lamb!" said the driver, in a voice that sounded far-off and rumbly. "Watch out, now! I'se gwine to frow it up de hole!"

"All right!" said Arnold. "I'll catch her!"

"No, don't throw my Lamb!" objected Mirabell. "She might fall on the sidewalk and break."

"All right—den I'll HAND her up out ob de hole," called the colored man, who was now in the partly filled bin under the sidewalk. "Watch out fo' her!"

Mirabell and Arnold could hear him walking around on the coal under the sidewalk. In another half minute a black hand was thrust up through the hole, and in the hand was a white, woolly Lamb on Wheels. Wait a minute! Did I say white? Well, I meant to have said a BLACK Lamb.

For Mirabell's white, clean Lamb on Wheels was now covered with black coal dust.

"Oh, that isn't my Lamb on Wheels at all!" cried Mirabell, and there were real tears in her eyes as her brother took the coal-dust covered toy from the colored man's hand. "That isn't my Lamb at all!"

"Oh, yes, it must be, Mirabell," said Dorothy's mother. "No other Lamb has fallen down the coal hole."

"But my Lamb was WHITE, and this one is BLACK," sobbed the little girl.

"Well, bring her in here and we'll wash her nice and clean and white again," said Dorothy's mother. "Bring your Lamb in, Mirabell. Dorothy is better now, though she cannot be out yet, and she will be glad to see you. Come in and I'll wash your Lamb!"

"And I certainly do need a bath!" thought the Lamb to herself, when she heard this talk. She could look down at her legs and see how black they were. "Oh, what a terrible adventure it is to fall into a coal hole! I wonder what will happen next!"

And she soon found out. For when the colored man had come out of the cellar, and was again shoveling the coal down the hole, Mirabell and Arnold took the black Lamb on Wheels into Dorothy's house. Dorothy and her brother Dick were glad to see the children from next door.

"Now to give Mirabell's Lamb a bath," said Dorothy's mother.

"I wonder if I'll be put in the bathtub, as the Wooden Lion was," thought the Lamb.

And she was, though she was not dipped all the way in, for fear of spoiling the wooden, wheeled platform on which she stood. With a nail brush and some soap and water, Dorothy's mother scrubbed the coal dust out of the Lamb's wool.

"There, she is nice and clean again," said Dorothy's mother, as she held the Lamb on Wheels up for the four children to see.

"But she is all wet!" cried Mirabell.

"I'll set her down by the warm stove in the kitchen, and she will soon dry," said the mother of Dick and Dorothy.

"And I'll put my Sawdust Doll down there with the Lamb so she won't be lonesome," said Dorothy.

And then the four children played games in the sitting room, while waiting for the Lamb to dry. And as Mary, the cook, was not in the kitchen just then, the Lamb and the Sawdust Doll were left alone together for a time.

"Oh, my dear, how glad I am to see you again!" exclaimed the Sawdust Doll when they were alone. "But, tell me! what happened? You are soaking wet!"

"Yes, it's very terrible!" bleated the Lamb. "I fell down a coal hole and had a bath!"

Then she told her different adventures, and the Sawdust Doll told hers,

so the two toys had a nice time together. Soon the warm fire made the

Lamb nice and dry and fluffy again. And she was as clean as when jolly

Uncle Tim, the sailor, had bought her in the store.

"How is the White Booking Horse?" asked the Lamb of the Doll, when they had finished telling each other their adventures.

"Oh, he's just fine!" exclaimed the Sawdust Doll. "Did you hear about his broken leg, how he went to the Toy Hospital, and how he scared away some burglars by kicking one downstairs?"

"No, I never heard all that news," said the Lamb. "Please tell me," and the Sawdust Doll did. Then the two toys had to stop talking together as Mirabell, Arnold, Dorothy and Dick came into the kitchen.

"Oh, now my Lamb is all nice again!" cried Mirabell, when she saw her toy. "Oh, I am so glad."

"So am I," said Dorothy.

For many days Mirabell had jolly good times with her Lamb on Wheels.

Sometimes the Lamb was taken to Dorothy's house, and then there was a

chance for the woolly toy to talk to the Sawdust Doll and the White

Rocking Horse.

And one day the Lamb had another strange adventure.

Mirabell had been out in the street near Dorothy's house drawing her Lamb up and down by means of a string. And Mirabell kept watch to see that Carlo did not run along and get tangled in the string. The little girl also made sure that no sidewalk coal holes were open. She did not want the Lamb to fall into another one.

"Oh, Mirabell, come over here a minute!" called Dorothy to her friend.

"Mother got me a new trunk for my Sawdust Doll's things."

"Oh, I want to see it!" cried Mirabell, and she was in such a hurry that she let go of the string by which she had been by herself on the sidewalk for a little way, and finally rolled out toward the gutter. For once in her life Mirabell forgot all about her toy, pulling her Lamb. The Lamb rolled along.

[Illustration: Lamb On Wheels Tells Sawdust Doll of Her Troubles]

And while Mirabell was looking at the new trunk for the Sawdust Doll's clothes, a big dog came running along the street. He saw the white, woolly Lamb near the curbstone.

"Oh, ho! Maybe that is good to eat!" thought the dog. And before the Lamb on Wheels could say a word, that dog just picked her up in his mouth and carried her away as a mother cat carries her little ones. Yes, the big dog carried away the Lamb on Wheels!

CHAPTER VIII

SAILING DOWN THE BROOK

The Lamb on Wheels was so frightened when the dog took her up in his mouth that she did not know what to do. If she could, she would have rolled away as fast as a toy railroad train, such a train as Arnold and Dick played with. But the dog had the Lamb in his mouth before she knew what was happening.

Besides, across the street was a man, and, as he happened to be looking at the Lamb, of course she dared not make believe come to life and trundle along as she sometimes did in the toy store. It was against the rules, you know, for any of the toys to do anything by themselves when any human eyes saw them. And so the Lamb had to let herself be carried away by the dog.

Now you might think that when the man saw the dog run away with the Lamb on Wheels in his mouth the man would have stopped the dog. But the man was thinking of something else. He was looking for a certain house, and he had forgotten the number, and he was thinking so much about that, and other things, that he never gave the Lamb a second thought.

He did see the dog take her away, but maybe he imagined it was only some game the children were playing with the toy and the dog, for Mirabell and Dorothy were there on the street, in plain sight.

But as the two little girls were just then thinking of the new trunk for the Sawdust Doll, neither of them thought of the Lamb, and they did not see the dog take her.

"Oh, what a nice trunk!" said Mirabell to Dorothy.

"I'm glad you like it," said Dorothy. She had her Sawdust Doll in her arms, and, as it happened, the Doll saw the dog running away with the Lamb on Wheels in his mouth.

"Oh! Oh! Oh, dear me! That is dreadful!" said the Sawdust Doll to herself. "Oh, the poor Lamb! What will happen to her?"

Away ran the dog with the Lamb on Wheels in his mouth down the street, over a low fence, and soon he was in the vacant lots where the weeds grew high. And then, as there were no human eyes in the vacant lots to see her, the Lamb thought it time to do something. She began to wiggle her legs, though she could not get them loose from the platform with wheels on, and she cried out:

"Baa! Baa! Baa!"

"Hello there! what's the matter?" barked the dog, and it made his nose tickle to have the Lamb, whom he was carrying in his teeth, give that funny Baa! sound in his mouth.

"Matter? Matter enough I should say!" exclaimed the Lamb on Wheels. "Why are you carrying me away like this, you very bad dog?"

For, being a toy, she could talk animal language as well as her own, and the dog could understand and talk it, too.

"Why am I carrying you away?" asked the dog. "Because I am hungry, of course."

"But I am not good to eat," bleated the Lamb. "I am mostly made of wood, though my wheels are of iron. Of course I have real wool on outside, but inside I am only stuffed."

"Dear me! is that so?" asked the dog, opening his mouth and putting the

Lamb down amid a clump of weeds in the vacant lot.

"Yes, it's just as true as I'm telling you," went on the Lamb. "I am only a toy, though when no human eyes look at me I can move around and talk, as can all of us toys. But I am not good to eat."

"No, I think you're right about that," said the dog, after smelling of the Lamb. For that is how dogs tell whether or not a thing is good to eat—by smelling it.

"You looked so natural," went on the dog, "that I thought you were a real little Lamb. That's why I carried you off when that little girl left you and ran away. I'm sorry if I hurt you."

"No, you didn't hurt me, but you have carried me a long way from my home," the Lamb said. "I don't know how I am ever going to get back to Mirabell."

"Can't you roll along to her on your wheels?" asked the dog. "I haven't time now to carry you back."

"Not very well," the Lamb answered. "It is very rough going in this lot, full of weeds and stones. I can easily roll myself along on a smooth floor, in the toy shop or at Mirabell's home. But it is too hard here."

"Ill leave you here now," barked the dog, "and when it gets dark I'll come and get you. I'll carry you back to the porch of the house, from in front of which I carried you off. Then you can roll in and get back to Mirabell, as you call her. Shall I do that?"

"Well, I suppose that would be a good plan," the Lamb said. "I don't exactly like being carried in your teeth, but there is no help for it."

"Then I'll do that," promised the dog. "I'll come back here and get you after dark. You'll be all right here in the tall weeds."

"I suppose so," replied the Lamb. "Though I shall be lonesome."

"Please forgive me for causing you all this trouble," went on the dog. "I never would have done it if I had known you were a toy. And now I'll run along and come back to-night. I hear a dog friend of mine calling me."

Another dog, at the farther end of the lot, was barking, and the Lamb crouched deeper down in the weeds.

"Dear me! this surely is an adventure," said the Lamb on Wheels to herself, as she was left alone. "Being taken away in a rag bag, as the Sawdust Doll was, couldn't be any worse than this. And though none of my legs is broken, as was one of the White Rocking Horse's, still I am almost as badly off, for I dare not move. I wonder what will happen to me next!"

It was not long before something did happen. As the Lamb stood on her wheels and wooden platform among the weeds, all at once two boys came along. They were looking for some fun.

"Oh, look!" cried a big boy. "There's a little white poodle dog over in the weeds!" and he pointed to the Lamb, whose white coat was easily seen amid the green leaves.

"Oh, we can have some fun with it!" said the little boy. "Let's call it."

So they whistled and called to the white object they thought was a dog, but the Lamb did not move. Of course she couldn't, while the boys were looking at her.

"That's funny!" said the big boy. "What do you think is the matter with that dog? It doesn't come to us."

"Let's go up and see," said the smaller lad.

Together they tramped through the weeds until they were close to the toy. Then the big boy cried out:

"Why, it isn't a dog at all! It's a Lamb on Wheels!"

"So it is!" said the little boy. "But I know how we can have some fun with it, just the same!"

"How?" asked the big boy.

"We can play Noah's Ark over in the brook," explained the small boy. "There are some boards over there. I was making a raft of them the other day. We can make another raft now, and we can get on and sail down the brook. And we can take the Lamb on board with us and make believe we're in a Noah's Ark and that there's a flood and all like that! Won't that be fun?"

"Yes, I guess it will," said the big boy. "Come on! I'll carry the

Lamb."

So, picking up the toy and tucking it under his arm, he led the way to the brook, which ran through the vacant lots. It was a nice brook, not too deep, and wide enough to sail boats on.

"Now we'll make the raft," said the smaller boy, as they came to a place on the bank of the brook where there were some boards and planks.

The big boy set the Lamb down near the water and then the two lads began to make a raft. A raft is like the big, wide, flat boat, without any house or cabin on it. It did not take long to make it.

"All aboard!" cried the big boy, when the raft had been finished. "All aboard! Come on!" He picked up the Lamb again, and walked out on the raft. The smaller boy went with his chum. With long poles, cut from a near-by tree, the boys shoved the raft out into the middle of the brook.

"Now we're a Noah's Ark!" laughed the small boy, "and we have one animal with us—a woolly Lamb on Wheels!"

And down the brook Mirabell's toy went sailing with the two boys on the raft.

"This is certainly surprising!" thought the Lamb. "I was bought by a sailor, and here I am making a voyage! I hope I shall not be seasick!"

CHAPTER IX

ON A LOAD OF WOOD

Now while the Lamb on Wheels was being carried away by the dog, and after she had been dropped in the lot, where she was picked up by the boys and put on a Noah's Ark raft—while all this was happening to the toy, Mirabell, the little girl who owned the Lamb, was almost heart-broken. After she had admired the trunk Dorothy had had given to her for the Sawdust Doll, Mirabell ran back to get her pet toy.

"Oh, where is my Lamb on Wheels?" cried Mirabell, looking up and down the street. "Where is she?"

"Where did you leave her?" asked Dorothy, who had gone back with her friend.

"I left the Lamb right here by the fence," answered Mirabell. "She had a string on. I was pulling her along the sidewalk, and when you called me I let go the string and ran. Oh, where is my nice Lamb?"

"Maybe Dick took the Lamb," suggested Dorothy to Mirabell, when they had looked up and down the street, in front of and behind the fence, and even in the yard, and had not found the toy. "Dick sometimes takes my things and hides them just for fun," Dorothy said.

"Or Arnold, maybe," added Mirabell.

Just then Dick and Arnold came out of Mirabell's house, each with a slice of bread and jam, and there was some jam around their mouths, too, showing that they had each taken a bite from their slices of bread.

"Oh, Arnold, did you take my Lamb!" cried Mirabell.

"Or did you take it, Dick?" asked his sister.

"Nope!" answered both boys, speaking at the same time.

"But where is she?" asked the little girl over and over again. "Where is my Lamb on Wheels?"

"Oh, I know!" suddenly cried Dick.

"I thought you said you didn't!" exclaimed his sister. "You said you and

Arnold didn't hide her away."

"Neither did we," went on Dick. "But I think I know where she is, just the same."

"Where?" asked Arnold, as he finished the last of his bread and jam, having given his sister a bite, while Dick gave Dorothy some. "Where is the Lamb on Wheels?" asked Arnold.

"Down in our cellar!" went on Dick. "Don't you remember how she rolled down there once, when the man was putting in coal? Maybe she's there again."

"Oh, let's look!" cried Mirabell.

So the children ran to Dorothy's mother, who said she would have

Patrick, the gardener, look down in the coal bin for the lost Lamb on

Wheels.

But of course the Lamb on Wheels was not in Dorothy's cellar, and

Mirabell felt worse than ever.

"I guess some one must have come along the street when you weren't looking, Mirabell," said Dorothy's mother, "and carried your Lamb away."

"I—I guess so," sobbed Mirabell. "Oh, but I wish I had her back. Uncle Tim gave her to me, and now he is away far out on the ocean! Oh, dear!" and the little girl felt very bad indeed.

She did not give up the search, and Dorothy, Dick and Arnold also helped. They looked in the two yards, across the street, and in other places, but the Lamb could not be found.

[Illustration: The Boys Leave Lamb on Wheels on the Raft]

The reason Mirabell could not find her toy, as you and I know very well, was because the Lamb on Wheels was riding down the brook on a raft with the two boys.

At first the Lamb was much frightened when she looked over the edge of the flat boat of planks and boards, and saw water on all sides of her.

"I really must be at sea, as that jolly sailor was," thought the Lamb. "I am on a voyage at last! Oh, I hope I shall not be seasick! Oh, how wet the ocean is!" she thought, as some water splashed up near her, when the little boy shoved the raft along with his pole.

The Lamb, not knowing any better, thought the brook was the big ocean.

But as the raft sailed on down and down and did not upset and as the

Lamb grew less frightened and was not made ill, she began to feel better

about it.

"Perhaps I am more of a sailor than I thought," she said to herself. "I never knew I would be brave enough to go to sea. I wish the Bold Tin Soldier and the Calico Clown could see me now. I'm sure they never had an adventure like this!"

So the Lamb on Wheels stood on her wooden platform in the middle of the raft and looked at the water of the brook. Now and then little waves splashed over the edge of the raft, but only a little water got on the toy, and that did not harm her.

"Isn't this fun!" cried the little boy who had first thought of playing

Noah's Ark with the raft.

"It is packs of fun!" agreed the older boy. "Let's make believe we are going on a long voyage."

So the raft went on and on down the brook, and the Lamb on Wheels was having a fine ride.

"Though I wish some of the toys were here with me," she thought to herself. "I wonder if the Sawdust Doll would get seasick if she were on board here. I don't believe the Bold Tin Soldier would, and the Calico Clown would be trying to think of new jokes and riddles, so I don't believe he would be ill. But I wonder what is going to happen to me? What will be the end of this adventure?"

The two boys poled their raft down to a broader part of the brook, where it flowed at the bottom of a garden. At the upper end of the garden was a large house, and not far away was another house. The Lamb on Wheels could see the houses from where she stood on the raft, and she wondered if any little boys or girls lived in them.

"Having adventures is all right," thought the Lamb, "but one can have too many of them. I have been on a voyage long enough, I believe. I wish I could get back home to Mirabell."

A few minutes after that the big boy cried:

"Oh, come on, Jimmie! There's Tom and Harry! We can have a game of ball," and he pointed to some boys who were running around the lots, through which the brook was now flowing.

"What shall we do with the Lamb?" asked the small boy.

"Leave it here on the raft," answered the older boy. "Maybe we'll want to play Noah's Ark again, and we can find the raft here. Now we'll go and play ball!"

They shoved the raft over toward the shore of the brook, and then the two boys jumped off. They left the Lamb behind them.

"Dear me! how fast things do happen," said the Lamb, speaking out loud to herself, as there was no one near just then. "A little while ago Mirabell was pulling me along the sidewalk with a string. Then she left me and the dog ran off with me. Then he left me, and the boys carried me off on the raft. Now they have left me. I wonder who will take me next?"

The raft was smooth in places, and the Lamb was just going to start to roll along a board toward shore when, all at once, she heard a noise, and a voice cried:

"Whoa!"

"My goodness!" thought the Lamb, coming to a stop almost as soon as she had started along on her wheels, "what's that? I wonder if some one is driving the White Rocking Horse along here!"

She looked through the weeds growing on the edge of the brook and saw a real horse and wagon and a real man driving down to the water through the vacant lot. And as the man was real the Lamb dared not move while he was in sight.

"Whoa!" called the real man, and it was to his real horse he was speaking, and not to the White Rocking Horse. "Whoa now, Dobbin!" went on the man, "and I'll let you have a drink here if the water is clean. I know you are thirsty, and there is a brook here somewhere."

So that is why the man was driving his horse down through the lot—to give his horse a drink. The man climbed down off his wagon and walked toward the brook, right at the place where the raft had gone ashore with the Lamb on board.

"I wonder if this can be the junkman who carried the Sawdust Doll away in his wagon," thought the Lamb. "If it is I am in for another adventure!"

As the man came to look at the brook, to see if the water was clean enough for his horse to drink, the man saw the raft.

"Oh, ho! There are some good boards and planks I can carry home to break up for kindling wood," said the man. "That's what I'll do. I'll have some good firewood from these boards! Or maybe I can sell some." Then he came nearer and saw the Lamb.

"Well, I do declare!" the man cried. "There is a white woolly Lamb toy! I must take that, too, though I don't know what I can do with it. Maybe I can sell it. I am in luck to-day, getting a load of wood and a toy. Now come on, Dobbin!" he called to his horse. "The brook is nice and clean for you to drink from, and while you are drinking I will load the wood on my wagon and take the Lamb on Wheels. Come on, Dobbin!"

The horse walked toward the water, for he was thirsty. And while he was drinking the man laid aside the Lamb, placing her on some soft grass.

Then he piled the boards and planks on his wagon, and next he took up the Lamb again, putting her on top of the load of wood.

"I'll give the Lamb a ride!" said the man.

CHAPTER X

MIRABELL IS HAPPY

Away rattled the wagon with the load of wood. The man sat on the seat, driving the horse, and behind him, where he had placed her on a board so she would not roll off, was the Lamb on Wheels.

"Are my adventures never going to end?" thought the Lamb. "Here I am riding on a wagon, while, a short time ago, I was on a raft, sailing over the ocean like Uncle Tim."

The Lamb did not know the difference between the brook and the ocean, but we can hardly blame her, as she had not traveled very much.

"I rather like this wagon ride, though," said the Lamb, as the man drove away from the brook and up through the lots. His horse was no longer thirsty.

The man who had picked up the pieces of the boys' raft to take home to be chopped up for firewood, did all sorts of odd jobs in the neighborhood. He would cut grass, beat rugs, cart away rubbish, and do things like that for people who lived near the brook. And soon after loading his wagon with wood and taking away the Lamb on Wheels the man said to himself:

"I'll go around to the Big House and ask if they have any trash that needs carting away. I can't take it now, because I have this load of wood on, but I could come to-morrow and get it. Yes, I'll drive to the Big House and see if they need me."

The "Big House," as the man called it, was a place where a gardener, a cook, and a maid were kept by a rich family, and the gardener used to rake up the trash in the yard and keep it until the rubbish man called with his wagon to take it away.

So along rattled the wagon with the Lamb on Wheels up on the pile of wood. She slid from side to side, as the road was now rough, and once she almost fell out. But the man looked around just in time and saw her.

"Oh, ho! Mustn't have that happen!" he exclaimed. "I don't want to lose the Lamb I found. It's an almost new toy, and maybe I can sell it. I must not lose it!"

Then he reached back and took the Lamb on Wheels from along the loose pieces of wood.

"I'll set it up on the seat beside me," said the man, talking aloud to himself, as he often did. "I can hold it on as we go over the rough places."

But soon the man drove out of the lots to a smooth road, and then the

Lamb felt better.

"Now we'll stop at the Big House," said the man, as he drove up along a back road and stopped at a gate in a high fence. "Whoa!" he called to his horse, and when the horse stopped the man got down off the seat, leaving the Lamb still there.

The man who had the load of wood opened the gate in the fence, and just then another man came out.

"Hello, Patrick!" called the wood man. "I was driving past and I just thought I'd stop and see if there was any trash you wanted carted off to the dump. Of course I can't take it now, as I have on a load of wood," he added. "But I can come back later."

"Oh, so you have a load of wood, have you?" asked Patrick, who had a garden rake in his hand. "Where did you get it?" and he walked toward the wagon, letting the garden gate swing shut behind him.

"Found it down in the lot near the brook. Some boys had made a raft, but

I guess they got tired of playing with it, so I took the planks and

boards. I found something else, too, Patrick!" "You did? What was that,

Mike?"

"A toy woolly Lamb on Wheels," answered the odd-job man. "It was on the raft. I brought it along with me. There it is, up on the seat," and he pointed to the toy.

"A Lamb! A toy Lamb on Wheels!" exclaimed Patrick. "Well, if this isn't strange! I never would have believed it!"

"What's the matter?" asked the odd-job man, as Patrick looked more closely at the Lamb on the wagon seat. "What's the matter?"

"Why, this is Mirabell's Lamb! The one she has been looking for!" cried Patrick. "I hunted down in our cellar for this Lamb, but I didn't find her. And now you have her on a load of wood! How strange! Where did you say you found her?"

"On the raft," answered the odd-job man. "But who is Mirabell?"

"A little girl who lives next door," explained Patrick, the gardener. "She plays with our Dorothy, and Mirabell's Uncle Tim brought her a Lamb on Wheels.

Mirabell had her Lamb out in the street, but she left it for a moment and then it disappeared. Now here it is!"

"Are you sure it's the same one?" asked the odd-job man.

"Quite sure," answered Patrick, and, oh, how the Lamb wished she dared speak out and say that she certainly was that very same toy! And how she wished they would take her to Mirabell!

"We can soon tell if this is Mirabell's Lamb," went on Patrick. "I'll take it to her. If you want to you can unload that wood here. My master will buy it and I can chop it up. Then you can cart away some trash in your wagon."

"I'll do that," said the odd-job man. "I guess the Lamb brought me good luck. I was thinking maybe I could sell this wood after I had chopped it up myself, but I'd rather sell it as it is. And I can then cart away the trash."

"Well, you be unloading the wood," said Patrick, "and I'll go see if this is Mirabell's Lamb. But I am very sure it is."

Leaning his rake up against the back fence, Patrick walked up the garden path, around the "Big House," as the odd-job man had called it, and then the gardener went toward the house where Mirabell lived.

The little girl, who had hunted all over for her Lamb on Wheels and was feeling very sad because she had not found it, was in the kitchen getting a cookie from Susan, the cook, when Patrick knocked on the back door.

"I'll go and see who it is!" cried the little girl.

And when she opened the door, and saw Patrick from the "Big House" standing there with the Lamb on Wheels, Mirabell was so surprised that she dropped her cookie. It fell on the floor, and it almost rolled down the back steps, but Patrick caught it in time.

"Oh! Oh!" exclaimed Mirabell, clasping her hands. "Where did you find her? Where did you find my Lamb on Wheels, Patrick?"

"Then she is yours?" asked the gardener.

"Of course she's mine!" cried Mirabell, as she took her toy in her arms.

"I've been looking everywhere for her! Oh, where did you find her?"

"I didn't find her. Another man did," explained the gardener. "But as soon as I saw this Lamb on the seat of his wagon, I thought she was yours. And she is!"

"Yes, she is!" cried Mirabell, who was very happy now. "This is my Lamb on Wheels, and I'm never going to lose her again. Oh, Patrick, I'm so glad!" she cried. "Will you thank the other man for me?"

"You may come and thank him yourself if you like," said the good-natured gardener. "He's unloading wood at our back gate, and he's going to take away a load of trash for me. Come and thank him yourself."

And Mirabell, holding the Lamb in her arms, did so.

"I can't tell you how glad and happy I am," said Mirabell.

"I am glad I happened to find your toy for you," replied the odd-job man.

Then, the little girl, nodding and smiling at Patrick and Mike, ran laughing across the yard to tell her mother the good news.

"I'm never going to lose my Lamb on Wheels again!" said Mirabell.

"I wonder where she was, and how she got on the raft by the brook," said Arnold, when he and Dick and Dorothy had heard the story of the finding of the lost toy.

"I don't know," answered Mirabell.

"All I know is that I have her back again, and, oh! I'm so happy!"

"I certainly am glad to get back to Mirabell again," said the Lamb on Wheels to herself. "And what a remarkable adventure I shall have to tell the Sawdust Doll and the White Rocking Horse when I see them again!"

This happened very soon, for a few days later Mirabell carried the Lamb on Wheels over to Dorothy's house. Arnold went with his sister, taking with him his toy fire engine.

"Now we'll have some fun!" cried Dick, as he got his White Rocking

Horse. "We'll go horseback riding."

"And I'll get my Sawdust Doll!" exclaimed Dorothy.

The children had fun playing with their toys, and when they laid them down for a moment to go to the kitchen to get some crackers and milk, the Lamb found a chance to tell the Sawdust Doll and the White Rocking Horse about her adventures.

"My, I think they are perfectly wonderful!" exclaimed the Doll, when she heard about the trip on the raft.

"But what is that little squeaky noise, Lamb?" asked the White Rocking

Horse suddenly. "I've noticed it every time you have moved."

"Oh, my dear!" cried the Sawdust Doll, "are you sure these dreadful adventures have not hurt you?"

"It's really not very much," answered the Lamb on Wheels. "You know an ocean trip such as mine is apt to be rather damp, and I have been left with a little rheumatism in my left hind wheel. But now that I am back with Mirabell it will soon be all right."

"She ought to have her mother put a little oil on it," said the Sawdust

Doll. "That would cure it at once."

"And did the odd-job man's horse go faster than I can go?" asked the

Rocking chap.

"I hardly remember," the Lamb answered. "But I was almost seasick riding on that wagon."

"Hush! The children are coming back!" neighed the White Rocking Horse, and the toys had to be very still and quiet.

"I know what we can do!" cried Dick, after he had helped Arnold put out a make-believe fire with the toy engine. "We can play soldier!"

"That will be fun!" said Arnold, who liked games of that sort. "I wish I had some toy soldiers," he went on. "I saw some in the same store where your Rocking Horse came from, Dick. I wish I had a set of tin soldiers, with a captain and a flag and everything!"

"Oh, I hope he does," thought the Lamb on Wheels. And if you children want to know whether or not Arnold got his wish you may find out by reading the next book in this series, called: "The Story of a Bold Tin Soldier."

As for the Lamb on Wheels, she lived with Mirabell for many, many years, and had a fine time. She had some adventures, too, but none more strange than the one of riding down the brook on a raft.

THE END